To Mommy and Daddy and Bettina
—with love from Lady

THE PERFECT RIDE

by Lady McCrady

pictures by Dennis Kendrick

PARENTS MAGAZINE PRESS
NEW YORK

Text copyright ©1981 by Lady McCrady.   Illustrations copyright ©1981 by Dennis Kendrick.
All rights reserved.   Printed in the United States of America.
10 9 8 7 6 5

Library of Congress Cataloging in Publication Data   McCrady, Lady. The perfect ride.
SUMMARY: While visiting Play Land one Saturday, Mommy
and Daddy Dog and their two children discover the perfect ride.
[1. Amusement parks—Fiction.   2. Dogs—Fiction.]   I. Kendrick, Dennis.   II. Title.
PZ7.M13813Pe   [E]   80-25612   ISBN 0-8193-1051-4   ISBN 0-8193-1052-3 (lib. bdg.)

It was Saturday at Play Land.

Mommy and Daddy Dog were there with their two children, Butchie and Queenie.

They'd been on the Merry-Go-Round,
and they'd eaten cotton candy.

They'd been to the
Wild West Fun House,

and they'd had their fortunes told.

"We have just four tickets left,"
Mommy Dog said.
"Enough for one last ride."
"It has to be perfect," Queenie said.
The Dogs looked all around them.

"This ride is keen," said Queenie.
"Yecch! I hate lizards," Daddy Dog said.
"And I won't ride a roller-skating one."
"How about the bumper cars?"
Mommy Dog said.
"They look racy and fast."
"Your driving is fast enough, dear,"
Daddy Dog said.

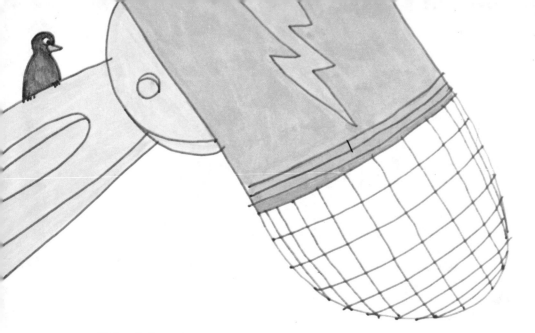

"Ooh! I know! Let's go on
the Space Bullet," said Daddy Dog.
"I'm not hanging upside down
when it gets stuck," Mommy Dog said.
"No way!"

"The Flying Snake is excellent!" Queenie said.
"I'm going to be sick," said Butchie.

Then they heard a girl yelling,
"Step this way, folks!
Take a boat ride to the
fantastic Bermuda Triangle!"
There were scary pictures
by the entrance.
There was strange music
coming from inside.

"Wow!" said Butchie.
"This ride looks perfect!" said Queenie.
Mommy Dog and Daddy Dog agreed.
The Dogs got in line for the ride.

They got into a boat.
"Hold on!" Daddy Dog said.
The boat slid into a dark tunnel.

"Woooo," sang Queenie.
"Wooooo," sang an echo.
"Shhh!" said Butchie.
"Shhhhh!" said the echo.

The music got louder.
Drums pounded.
The boat creaked.

"Look at that octopus," said Queenie.
"How about that pirate!" shouted Butchie.

Then the Dogs saw the entrance
to a tiny cave ahead.
Their boat floated through it...

U.S.S. LEEKEE

and stopped with a big bump!
"Boy, it's quiet in here," said Queenie.
"What happened to the music?"
"It's dark, too," whispered Butchie.
"I can't see a thing."

S.S. LEEKEE

Daddy Dog lit a match.
"How will we get out of this tunnel?"
he said.
"There's an EXIT sign over there,"
Mommy Dog said.
"I'm scared!" cried Butchie.

"What was THAT bump?" Daddy Dog said.
"I think another boat just hit us,"
Mommy Dog answered. "Some animal is
breathing down my neck!" Queenie yelled.

"Sorry," said a voice. "But there's no
way to stop this thing."
"Mommy, I'm scared," whined another voice.
Soon there were a bunch of voices in the dark.

"Oh, no! The water's filling up!"
Queenie yelled. "We'll all drown!"
"Let us out!" someone yelled.

"LET US OUT!" everyone in the tunnel yelled.
"LET US OUT!"

With a rush the boat started moving again.
"I thought we'd NEVER get out of THERE,"
Mommy Dog said.
"I'm glad THAT'S over," Daddy Dog said.

EKEE

"Oh, no, it isn't!" Queenie cried.
"Stop! Get me out of here!" Butchie said.
"Uh oh," they all said.

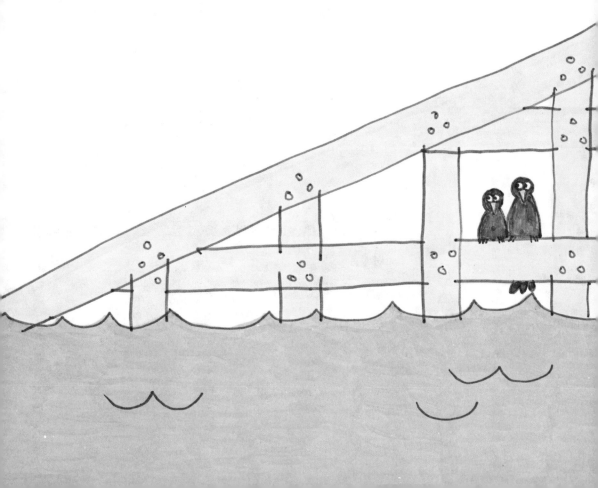

"NO, NO!" they cried.

YIPES!!

When the Dogs got off the ride,
there was a family watching them.
"How was it?" they asked.
"It was dark and spooky," said Butchie.
"We got stuck and then we got splashed."

"It sounds scary," said the family.
The Dogs smiled.
"It was," they said.
"It was THE PERFECT RIDE."

ABOUT THE AUTHOR

LADY MCCRADY is just under 5 feet tall and weighs less than 95 pounds, but she does more than enough for 10 big people! She is well known in libraries and schools as the author/ illustrator of 16 children's books. Her drawings appear in newspapers and magazines, and her paintings and other artwork have been widely exhibited. She talks at schools and has been on TV news and talk shows, and radio interviews.

Lady admits that she loves going to amusement parks when they are closed. "That's where my cat, Starboy, and I go roller skating," she says.

The Perfect Ride is the first book Lady has written for Parents.

ABOUT THE ILLUSTRATOR

DENNIS KENDRICK says he enjoyed illustrating *The Perfect Ride* because he loves amusement parks. He once worked as a ticket taker for a scary ride at Coney Island in Brooklyn. "Lots of people who went on it," he says, "came out with the same look on their faces that the Dog Family had!"

Dennis worked as a graphic designer in Connecticut until 1977, when he moved to New York City to work as a children's book illustrator. He has since illustrated books for many publishers, one of which he also wrote.

The Perfect Ride is the second book Dennis has illustrated for Parents, following *The Fox With Cold Feet,* written by Bill Singer.